The House
With No Name

by Pippa Goodhart

Illustrated by Peter Kavanagh

You do not need to read this page –
just get on with the book!

Published in 2003 in Great Britain by
Barrington Stoke Ltd
10 Belford Terrace, Edinburgh EH4 3DQ

This edition based on *The House With No Name*, published by Barrington
Stoke in 1999

Printed by Polestar AUP Aberdeen Ltd

MEET THE AUTHOR - PIPPA GOODHART

What is your favourite animal?
A dormouse
What is your favourite boy's name?
Mick
What is your favourite girl's name?
Tamla
What is your favourite food?
Fresh bread with butter and honey
What is your favourite music?
Mozart's Flute and Harp Concerto
What is your favourite hobby?
Mucking about with my family

MEET THE ILLUSTRATOR - PETER KAVANAGH

What is your favourite animal?
Grizzly bears
What is your favourite boy's name?
Poppa Bear
What is your favourite girl's name?
Momma Bear
What is your favourite food?
Porridge
What is your favourite music?
Let Me Be Your Teddy Bear
What is your favourite hobby?
Scratching

For Amy Winczkowski –
because she likes this story
P.G.

Contents

Chapter 1
The House

"What's the house like? Is it nice?" Jamie asked.

"You'll see very soon," said Jamie's dad.

"But can I have my own room?"

"A small one, yes. The girls will share the biggest bedroom and Mum and I will have the other."

Jamie sat smiling in the front seat. He had to sit with his sisters in the back if Mum was there. But now it was just him and his dad.

He had the map on his lap. The back of the van was full of tools and sleeping bags and food.

"So what *is* the house like? Mum says it's falling down!" said Jamie.

"We got a local chap to look at it and he says it's fine. We've just got to paint the place and put in the electrics. Then it'll feel like home! Now look out for a track on our left," Dad said.

They turned off the road and drove down a long tunnel of trees.

"This house is miles from anywhere!" said Jamie.

"You've got your bike," his father told him.

"It'll be dark at night," said Jamie. He was used to the street-lights in town. The thought of biking down this track after dark made him shiver.

Then the van bumped out of the tunnel of trees into the sunlight.

"There's our new home!" said Dad. "What do you think of it?"

Where? I can't see it!

It was the kind of house Jamie's sisters drew – a square with a door in the middle, a window at each corner and a high roof.

"It looks like a face!" said Jamie.

"Don't be silly!" said Dad and took the bag of tools from the van. "Now, have a quick look round and then come and help me carry this lot in."

The house did look like a face. The thatch on the roof was like hair. The two upstairs windows were like winking eyes. The windows downstairs had dark red planks over them. They looked like rosy cheeks. The red door was the mouth and the porch roof over it was the nose.

Jamie ran from empty room to empty room. The house felt alive. Jamie frowned and went to find his dad.

They went into the dimly-lit kitchen.
It looked clean and tidy.

Jamie's dad looked around, puzzled.
"You'd never think that there was an
explosion in this room, would you?"

"An explosion?" Jamie asked.

"Yes. Ages ago. Someone was killed."

Then Dad hung Jamie's cap over a nail on the back of the door. "There," he said, "as my old mum always said, *when you've hung up your cap, you're at home*. Shall we have a camp fire tonight?"

"Yeah, great!" said Jamie, smiling and putting his cap back on.

"But now we've got to mend this window." Dad took out his hammer.

"When was this explosion?" asked Jamie.

"About 35 years ago. A gas bottle blew up. The family left after that and the house has been empty ever since."

"Why did no one else want it?"

"Well," said Dad, "it's miles from anywhere. Houses like to have other houses around them."

Jamie grinned. "Now you're talking as if houses are people. And you said I was silly thinking the house looked like a face! Mum's the same. She said it needed to be cheered up.

Dad smiled. "She's right. It does feel sad."

"Yes. Sort of frozen in time. It wants to be lived in again. But I like it."

"Good," said Dad. "Now go and fetch me a plank of wood to prop the door open, will you?"

As Jamie was looking inside the van for the plank, a cold shiver went down his spine. He felt he was being watched.

He spun around to look. There was nothing there.

That's odd, he thought, and hurried back into the house with the plank.

Jamie kept Dad talking. Then he could forget that scary feeling that someone was watching him.

"I've always wanted to live in a wood," said Dad.

"Why?" asked Jamie.

"When I was little, we always lived in towns. We moved house a lot. I longed to settle in the country. I had to wait a long time. But when Gran died last year and left us some money, I found this place. And here we are," Dad said.

Jamie could remember his gran and grandad. Grandad was small and sad and wore a flat cap. Gran made lovely iced cakes.

"They were always moving house to escape from their sadness. You see, I had a brother who died. Your gran and grandad loved him so much," said Dad.

"More than they loved you?" asked Jamie.

"They didn't want me to think that. They didn't like to talk about him, but I always felt that he'd been closer to them."

"Dad," began Jamie, "I'll have to make new friends now, won't I? And we haven't even got an address or a phone number yet!"

"We'll soon sort that. What shall we call the house? Woodside? Or Rose Cottage?"

"Boring," said Jamie. "It needs a better name than that."

"What then?"

"I'll think about it," said Jamie.

Jamie and his dad worked all morning, mending the kitchen windows. Again, Jamie felt that he was being watched, but he saw no one.

"Did you hear something just then?" he asked his dad.

"No," his dad said.

Jamie was sure that someone out there was looking in at him. "I'll tell you a joke, Dad," he said at last. "What has the bottom at its top?"

"Dunno. I give up," his dad said.

Then a voice from outside the house
said, "Easy! A leg has a bottom at its top!"

A boy was looking in at the window and
he was laughing.

Chapter 2
Colin

"Hello," said the boy. "Are you like the others who came to look around or are you really going to live here?"

"Hi," said Dad. "Jamie and I are doing a bit of work on the house before the rest of the family gets here. He was just asking if there might be any other lads living round here. Do you live quite close?".

"Yes," said the boy.

He wore a shirt like Jamie's PE shirt from school, jeans and brown lace-up shoes. He had red cheeks and untidy blond hair. He made Jamie think of someone.

He wanted to ask the boy if he'd been watching them all morning. But all he said was, "Do you know any other jokes?"

The boy grinned. "What's black and white and black and white and black and white?"

"I don't know."

"A penguin rolling down a hill!" said the boy.

"What's this?" said Jamie. He wagged his little finger.

"A worm?" asked the boy.

"No! A microwave!"

"A what?" asked the boy, puzzled.

"Don't you get it? A microwave. You know, a very small wave!"

"Oh." The boy looked blank.

"Don't you have microwave ovens around here?" asked Jamie.

It was clear that the boy didn't know what Jamie was talking about. Perhaps they lived in the past around here, thought Jamie.

His dad winked at him. Then he smiled at them both. "I'll leave you two jokers to it and I'll fetch us all some lunch. I saw a fish and chip shop in the village. Would you like to have lunch with us?" he asked the boy.

The boy smiled. "Yes, please. I haven't had fish and chips for years and years and years!"

"What's your name?" asked Jamie.

"Colin."

"How old are you?"

"Eleven. I should have been twelve soon."

"Should have been?" said Jamie. "Going to be, you mean. Same as me! I'll be twelve next week. Have you lived around here long?"

"Yes, years and years," said Colin.

"Who were the *others* you said came to look around the house?" Jamie asked him.

"They wanted to knock down this house and build a new one." Colin seemed angry.

"So why didn't they?" asked Jamie.

"They gave up and went."

"Oh." Jamie thought that Colin was a bit odd, but he was the right age and a boy. Anyway, he was someone to do things with. "Which school are you at?" he asked. "I'm going to the local Comp. next term."

"I'm at the Grammar School," said Colin. "I had to pass exams to get in. I wanted to be an astronaut. Don't you think it would be great to land on the moon? They're planning to do that, you know!"

"Don't be silly!" said Jamie. "They did that years ago! It's Mars they want to land on now."

"You'd see the world from far away and you'd be free!" Colin went on.

"I think you're nuts!" said Jamie. "It'd be too lonely."

"It'd be beautiful. You'd see the world like a tiny ball in the sky."

"But Earth would be just a far-away dot. Wouldn't that scare you?" asked Jamie.

"It'd be worth it, to escape," said Colin, sadly.

"Escape from what?" Jamie thought of his gran and grandad and their sad life – always moving on. "You can't escape from your feelings by going away. They always go with you."

Chapter 3
Trouble

"Fish and chips coming up," called Jamie's dad as he stepped out of the van.

Jamie was glad to see food and to have Dad back.

"Sit down on that log and we'll eat them out of the paper, the proper way."

Dad looked over at Colin. "Do you need to ring your mum and tell her where you are?"

Colin shook his head. "No one will miss me." He held up a chip and then ate it slowly, his eyes closed. "Mmm!"

Jamie laughed, "It's only a chip, you know!" Then he said to his dad, "Guess what? Colin wants to be an astronaut!"

"Or a bird," said Colin. "I just want to be free to go up and away."

Colin knew all about the birds and animals and plants.

"Why don't you take Jamie into the wood and show him around?" said Dad. "I'll finish the windows. My mate is coming tomorrow to help me wire up the electrics. There's not much more we can do before then.

You go and explore. Bring back some dry sticks for a camp fire. Are you going to join us for sausages, Colin?"

"I'd like that," said Colin.

Colin led Jamie into the wood. "I'll show you where to find fir cones to get the fire started.

****

The wood all looked very much alike to Jamie, lots of trees and bracken and paths leading everywhere.

"I'd soon get lost in here," he said.

So Colin showed him how to work out where he was by checking where the sun was in the sky. Then he showed Jamie lots of plants and birds. He pointed out the tracks that the animals had made.

"And look at these!" said Colin. "D'you know what these are?"

"Yes, I do know. Nettles!" said Jamie. But Colin was pointing to something on one leaf.

"See that? Butterfly eggs. Just hatching."

"Blimey! The caterpillars are tiny!"

"Sometimes I feel like a caterpillar," said Colin. "But I'd like to be a butterfly. I'd have to make a cocoon for myself first."

"You do say some odd things," said Jamie.

"Have you ever watched a butterfly hatch out from a cocoon?" asked Colin.

Jamie shook his head.

"I have. They come out all folded up. They look as if they'd never be able to fly. But the sun warms them and that makes them stretch their wings out wide. Then they flap their wings and they're off." Colin gave a sigh.

"So you really do want to fly?" asked Jamie.

"More than anything. I want to go, up and away and be free," said Colin. "See that?"

He pointed to some tall, pink flowers. "I call it the rocket plant. They look like rockets ready to take off. Aren't they great?"

Jamie looked at Colin to see if he was joking. None of his old friends would have talked about flowers. But Colin wasn't joking. And he was right. The flowers were lovely.

"What's that?" asked Jamie as something laughed in the trees.

"Only a woodpecker," said Colin. "Don't you know any bird noises? You do have birds in town, don't you?"

"Yes," replied Jamie. "Pigeons and sparrows. And I know what cuckoos sound like."

"I hate cuckoos," said Colin. "They lay their eggs in other birds' nests. The poor mother bird has to go on feeding the great big cuckoo chick, even when it gets bigger than her. And it pushes her own chicks out of the nest."

Colin stopped to pick up a stick. Then he said, "I called my little brother Cuckoo. He was adopted."

"I've only got sisters," said Jamie.

"Cuckoo was a baby when he came to us. Mum and Dad thought he was great. He took up all of Mum's and Dad's time so there was none left for me."

"Didn't you like him at all?"

"Oh, yeah! As he grew bigger I showed him things – how to swing himself, that kind of thing. I loved him. And I hated him. You know."

Jamie laughed. "I know."

Then Colin looked at Jamie hard. "Have you ever really hated somebody – even just for a second? And did you tell them you hated them? Did you even say that you wished they were dead?"

Jamie nodded. "Yes. You can hate someone for doing something, but still love them. It gets mixed up."

"That's it! It was like that with me," shouted Colin.

"What do you mean?" asked Jamie.

Colin pointed to an old log. "See the marks on that?"

Jamie could see marks cut into the log.

"There's a *C* and a *T*," Colin told him.
"A *C* for me and a *T* for my brother. I let my brother use my knife to make his *T*. He was too little and he cut himself ... And I think I killed him."

"You what?" Jamie felt cold.

"I think I killed my brother."

"*Did* you kill your brother?" asked Jamie.

"I think so. I don't know!"

"Then go home and find out!" said Jamie. "I bet he's fine! Is that why you ran away?"

Colin felt the *C* and the *T* in the wood with his finger.

Jamie saw that the marks were old.
"Look, if things are in a mess, you can stay with us tonight," said Jamie. "Dad'll sort it all out for you. He's got his mobile with him."

Colin looked puzzled but said nothing.

They found some sticks for the camp fire. Then, Colin gave a sudden yell and put his hands to his head.

"What's up?" asked Jamie.

Colin looked at his hands in horror. His fingers held a small tuft of hair.

"How did that happen?" said Jamie.

With a wild cry Colin ran towards the house. What was the matter? Was he feeling ill?

There was a sudden shout and a terrible crash. Jamie ran after Colin.

"Dad!"

Chapter 4
Dad

An empty ladder was leaning against the house. Colin stood below it, his hands pressed to his mouth as if he was trying not to scream.

On the ground lay Jamie's dad.

"Dad! What happened? Are you hurt?" Jamie was scared. He put a hand on his dad's arm.

Dad opened his eyes. He was shaking. "My leg," he said. Then he closed his eyes again as the pain hit him.

"Don't move!" Jamie told him. "You might have hurt your back."

Dad's right leg was bent at a funny angle. "Colin, go and ring for an ambulance. Quick!" he said.

Colin ran off.

"What happened?" Jamie asked his dad.

"I was up the ladder, just pulling out a bit of thatch from the roof. Then something made me fall."

"Was it Colin? Did he do it?"

"No! Colin came running from the wood as I fell. He was shocked, poor lad."

"You might have died …"

"I know, Jamie. But I didn't and I'm not going to. It's just my leg that's bad. You'll have to get hold of your mum and go back home."

Jamie held his dad's hand. He told him they'd make the house into the best home ever. Then, at last, the ambulance came.

The ambulance men lifted Dad onto a stretcher and put him into the ambulance.

"Will he be all right?" asked Jamie.

"He'll be fine, but what about you?" asked the ambulance man.

"I'm going to ring my mum and go back home."

"Good boy."

They drove off down the bumpy track.

As they drove away, Jamie felt awful. "Show me where the phone box is, Colin. I've got to ring my mum."

"Why not stay here?" asked Colin.

"On my own?" said Jamie. He was shocked.

"I'll be here," Colin told him.

"Do you think Mum would let me?"

Jamie rang home and asked Mum if he could stay with a friend. He didn't tell his mum that he would be alone in the house with Colin.

"Has Dad met Colin?" she asked him.

"Yes. He likes him," Jamie told her.

"All right then. I'll pick you up tomorrow. Where does Colin live?"

"Don't worry about that, Mum. I'll be at our new house when you come over."

"OK, love. Take care. Bye!"

Chapter 5
Camp Fire

"Have you run away from home?" Jamie asked Colin. "I've thought about doing that."

"I'm not where I should be," Colin told him.

Jamie smiled, "So I'm going to spend a night with a ghost and a runaway!"

"Why do you say there's a ghost?" asked Colin.

"Somebody told my mum there was one."

"You don't seem to mind."

"I don't." Now, with Colin here, the place didn't seem spooky.

"Let's light the fire," said Colin.

"Good idea. The matches are in the van. There's also some bread and ketchup and drinks. Dad even remembered the tin opener for the beans."

Colin knew about making camp fires. "I was in the Scouts," he told Jamie, as the flames shot up from the sticks.

"Hungry?" asked Jamie.

"Starving!" said Colin. "I've not had a sausage for years and years!"

"You're always saying you haven't had something for years and years!" said Jamie.

Colin looked up at the house. "You told me he wasn't going to hurt the house, but he was pulling it to bits!"

"He only pulled out a tiny bit of thatch. What's wrong with that?"

Colin stared up at the thatch and put a hand to his head.

He's getting all odd again, thought Jamie. "You butter the bread and I'll open the beans," he told Colin.

As they ate, it began to get dark. The fire died down. "I'll take the torch and get the sleeping bags from the van," said Jamie.

Chapter 6
Ghosts?

They laid the sleeping bags on the floor of the front bedroom. They did not bother to wash or undress.

Jamie could hear noises all around. The house creaked and its pipes hummed. The wind blew down the chimney.

A sudden yipping sound made Jamie gasp.

"Only a fox outside," said Colin. "Sometimes they sound like a small boy yelling."

"It's all right," said Jamie. "I didn't think it was a ghost. I don't think this house is spooky."

Colin said nothing, so Jamie asked, "Do you think there are ghosts?"

"Yes."

"Are you sure?!" Jamie switched on his torch to see Colin's face.

"I know that you don't believe in ghosts," said Colin. "But the ghosts believe in you."

"Oh, ha ha! Are you trying to scare me?"

"No."

Jamie sat up in his sleeping bag and waved his torch around the room. "I can zap all the ghosts with this," he said.

Jamie shone the torch into Colin's face again. His skin was so pale you could almost see through it.

"You look as if you've seen a ghost!" said Jamie.

"I have. Lots of times."

"What, here?" asked Jamie.

"Yes," Colin told him. He wasn't joking.

Jamie almost choked. "What's it like then, this ghost? How old is it?" he said.

"About our age," said Colin.

"No! I mean, when did it live? Does it clank about in armour or a long dress or what? Does it wail and walk through walls?"

"No."

"Then what? What does its face look like?" Jamie wanted to know.

"I can't tell you. I haven't seen its face."

"A ghost without a head?" Jamie laughed.

"No." Colin looked at Jamie. "If you like, I'll tell you about it."

"Go on, then," said Jamie.

So Colin began. "There was once a man and woman who loved each other. They lived in this house in the wood and they wanted children."

"Is this a fairy story?" asked Jamie.

"D'you want to hear it, or not?"

"Yeah. Go on."

"Well, they had a baby boy. He grew up and went to school and learnt to swim and went fishing. The man and woman waited nine years for another baby, but none came. So they asked the boy if he would like them to adopt a baby.

"The boy knew how much his mum and dad wanted another baby, so he said *yes*. It came and it was a boy.

"The baby took the first boy's toys," Colin went on. "He cried all night. Mum and Dad were always busy looking after him. There was no time for any more fishing trips.

"Mum was always feeding the baby or cleaning him or playing with him. Dad worked hard to pay for the extra things they needed. So the bigger boy felt left out."

"Was the baby called Cuckoo?" asked Jamie.

"Yes." Colin's face was paper pale. "The one I killed."

"He cut himself with your knife by mistake?"

"No. It wasn't then. I killed him later, and it wasn't a mistake. I did mean to hurt him, but not to kill him." Colin's eyes were wide with pain.

Jamie put a hand on Colin's knee.

"How did it happen?" he asked.

"Cuckoo was four years old. One day he went into my room and he took the model rocket I'd made. He took it and he got Mum's rolling pin and he hit it and hit it and hit it. It was smashed to bits. When I found what he'd done, I wanted to smash him."

"I'd have felt just the same," said Jamie, but Colin didn't hear him.

"Cuckoo was out on the swing under the ash tree. He saw me and he shouted for me to look how high he could go. He didn't understand how angry I was about the

smashed rocket. I wanted so badly to hurt him, to make him cry like I was crying."

"You're crying now."

"It was easy to kill him." Colin said. "I just shouted his name, and waved."

"Waved?"

"Yes. With both hands. You see, we had a game where I did something – held my nose or hopped on one leg or something – and he'd copy it back. This time I waved with both hands and he copied me. That made him fall off the swing."

"Then what happened?"

"I saw him fall. I was happy. Then he landed on the ground and yelled. The next moment my hate exploded and we were all dead."

"Hate doesn't explode!" Jamie froze. "When was this, Colin?"

"I killed Cuckoo in 1965."

"Dad told me that a gas bottle exploded here in 1965. One person died, but I don't think ..."

Colin put his hands over his ears. "No! Don't tell me! I can't bear it!" He was shaking. "Everything stopped when my hate exploded! I don't want to know what happened next! I've kept things the same here for years and years and years ..."

"You scared away anyone who came here?"

"Yes!" said Colin.

"Did you make my dad fall off the ladder?" asked Jamie.

"I don't know. Maybe! I didn't want to, but I'm bad. I kill things. Your dad was pulling out my hair when he pulled out the thatch. It hurt me. I shouted for him to stop, but that was all!"

Colin's eyes were sad. "I think I can kill people without coming near them, Jamie. I did that to Cuckoo and to my mum and dad. And now your dad."

"My dad's not dead, Colin."

Then something clicked in Jamie's mind. "Did you say that Dad was pulling out your hair?"

"Yes. Pulling out great tufts of it."

"Colin, is this house you?" Jamie asked very softly.

Colin nodded. "Yes. That's how I've been able to keep it like it was. The house is me. And I'm the ghost."

Chapter 7
Exploding Free

What Colin had said still didn't make sense. "My Dad said that only one person died when the gas exploded. And it was nothing to do with anyone hating anyone else."

"I was there," said Colin. "So I know. My hate exploded and killed Terry and my parents."

"Who?" Jamie sat up. "What name did you say, Colin?"

"Terry."

"Is that Cuckoo's real name?"

"Yes."

"My dad's called Terry!"

"So what?"

Jamie got out of his sleeping bag and went over to Colin. "My dad was adopted too," he said. "Did your brother Terry have dark hair like my dad? Is your family name Hall?"

Colin sat up. Jamie could see in his eyes that the answer was yes.

"Then my dad must be your brother!" shouted Jamie. "He must be! And he's alive and his mum and dad were alive until not long ago. My gran – your mum – only died last year. You were the only one killed when the gas exploded."

Jamie jumped up from his sleeping bag and went over to the window. It was just getting light. Out in the yard, a small boy swung to and fro under the big ash tree.

Sunlight shone through the window. It shone right through Colin as if he wasn't there and lit up the floor under him.

Colin had no shadow.

Jamie went over to him. He put out a hand to touch Colin but there was nothing there. "Don't go, Colin. Look out of the window. There's Cuckoo on the swing!"

The small boy was tipping back and forth to work himself higher.

"Just watch," Jamie told Colin. "You'll see he'll be OK."

It was like watching a silent film.

The boy on the swing looked up at the house and shouted. His mouth was open, but there was no sound. He let go the ropes of the swing and waved with both hands. Then he fell.

"Quick!" Jamie ran down the stairs, dragged open the door and raced over to the small child.

Colin's mum and dad were there already. The little boy sat up. He was crying. Terry's and Colin's parents held out their arms to the child. At that same moment there was a terrible booming sound and Jamie was thrown to the ground.

For a moment Jamie lay, stunned and unable to think. But as he came to, he knew what that booming sound was even before he looked.

"Colin!" he shouted. "Colin, your mum and dad didn't die. You saved them! When Terry fell they ran outside so they weren't in the house when the gas exploded. You didn't kill anybody, Colin. You saved them all, and they loved you always!"

Jamie looked up. He was alone. Little Terry and his parents had gone.

Jamie saw that the house that had been Colin had exploded. Colin was free. It was exciting. It was beautiful and terrible.

Jamie cried with both sadness and joy.

Chapter 8
Peace

Jamie sat, stunned. The house was just a pile of rubble. It lay there at peace. The main sound now was the song of the birds.

"Are you free now, Colin?" Jamie asked the air.

The house felt at peace, the house that had been Colin. All the sadness had gone and the sun was shining.

Jamie wiped away his tears and got up.

Then he ran into the wood and found the place where the pink rocket flowers grew. He picked and picked them until his hands were sore and his arms were full.

He took the flowers back to the house that had been Colin.

He found where the fireplace had been. Part of the chimney still stood among the rubble.

He stuck the rocket flowers into the broken chimney as if it were a vase. Then he stood looking up into the sky and thought of birds and butterflies and people. He thought of space rockets.

"Goodbye, Colin," he said. "I'll tell Dad – tell Cuckoo – about you. We'll make a new house and live here always."

Colin will always be part of my life

And Jamie knew that he would find Colin in the birds and flowers and stars around their new home.

Colin would be a part of this place for ever.

Who is Barrington Stoke?

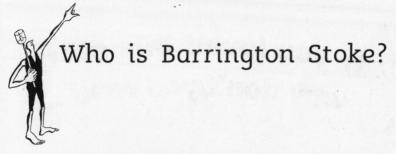

Barrington Stoke went from place to place with his lamp in his hand. Everywhere he went, he told stories to children. Some were happy, some were sad, some were funny and some were scary.

The children always wanted more. When it got dark, they had to go home to bed. They went to look for Barrington Stoke the next day, but he had gone.

The children never forgot the stories. They told them to each other and to their children and their grandchildren. You see, good stories are magic and they can live for ever.

If you loved this story, why don't you read ...

Life Line

by Rosie Rushton

Have you ever told a fib because it was easier than the truth? Skid finds himself in trouble because he tells one fib too many. But how can he tell the truth about his home life?

4u2read.ok!